Meep Comes to Earth

HEATHER BUTLER

Illustrated by Nick Ward

SCRIPTURE UNION

For the one who looks to see who my books are dedicated to. This one is for you.

By the same author
Message in a Bottle

© Heather Butler

First published 1999

Scripture Union, 207–209 Queensway, Bletchley, Milton Keynes, MK2 2EB, England.

ISBN 1 85999 320 6

British Library Cataloguing-in-Publication Data.
A catalogue record of this book is available from the British Library.

Printed and bound in Great Britain by
Creative Print and Design (Wales), Ebbw Vale.

Contents

Chapter 1

In the beginning...

It was Saturday afternoon and two boys were kicking a ball around in the park. On Monday they were playing for the school under-ten football team in the first round of the knock-out cup.

"I'm glad Mr Bradbury put you up front," Robert said, as Billy booted the ball high in the air.

"Yup. And Philip is centre half," Billy grinned. "If that doesn't scare the other team, nothing will!"

Robert pulled a face at the mention of Philip Hobson. He was the tallest boy in the class and a bully with it. Worse still, he had been chosen to be captain of the football team.

"You should have been made captain," Robert said. "You'd be much better than him."

Billy shrugged his shoulders. He was more bothered about getting a new pair of football boots. His dad was meant to be getting them for him. But Billy never knew when he was going to see his dad because he did not live with him and his mum any more.

"Hope my dad comes over tomorrow with my new boots," he said.

"And if *you* get a new pair of boots," Robert sighed, "Philip will have to have a new pair as well, won't he? He doesn't half get on my nerves."

"He's not *that* bad," Billy said.

He knew Philip better than Robert. They lived in the same road and Billy sometimes went to his house to play on his computer and play station. He liked that because Philip had more games than anyone else, and a room all to himself.

There was silence for a few minutes apart from the thudding of the football being booted around.

"I've had enough," Billy suddenly said,

bending down to pick the ball up. "Shall we go?"

Robert nodded. He was starting to get cold.

As Robert opened the back door a few minutes later he bumped into his dad.

"I'm going to see if they've got any new films at the video shop," Dad said. "D'you want to come and get one for you and Jack?"

"Ooh, yes," Robert said. "Hope they've got something good in."

They had.

In the children's section was 'The Return of Dinky Robot'.

Robert picked it up.

"That other 'Dinky Robot' film we had out was brill," Robert said. "Can we get this one?"

"Okay," Dad said, glancing down at the cassette case his son was clutching. "I've chosen my video as well."

"'Mr Finger's Downfall'," Robert read out loud. "'A romantic comedy set in the

Wild West'. Can I stay up and watch it with you?" He knew the answer before he asked the question, but it was worth a try.

"No!" Dad said. "You're only nine and you'll get bored."

Robert sighed.

He did not think he would get bored at all.

At that moment the shop door opened. Philip Hobson strutted in and headed for the rack of videos by the counter.

"Hello, Philip," Dad said as they, too, headed for the counter.

"Hello, Mr Gibson," Philip said back.

Robert did not like his dad being friendly towards Philip. Dad knew lots and lots of people because of his job as a milkman. When he collected his money on a Thursday evening he always called at Philip's house. Philip sometimes opened the door and paid him because his parents had gone out. That worried Dad who thought nine-year-olds were too young to be left on their own, especially when it was dark.

"Which video are you getting out then?"
Dad asked Philip now.

"Dunno," Philip sighed. "Mum and Dad
are busy tonight so they've given me some
money and said I can get whatever I want."

"Hope you find something good," Dad
said.

"I nearly asked Philip if he wanted to
come round to us this evening," he said a
few minutes later.

"No way!" Robert said. "I'm not having *him* coming to our house."

"Don't you feel sorry for him?" Dad asked. "He's going to be on his own all evening."

"That's his hard luck," Robert said. "He's a bully and I don't like him. At all."

"Maybe he's unhappy inside, and that's how he shows it," Dad commented. "His mum and dad don't seem to bother much with him."

They reached the front of their house and turned in to the drive. A grey blob suddenly darted across the garden. It sat by the door, waiting for them.

"You coming inside too?" Robert asked, scooping the cat up in his arms. Misty purred and gently rubbed his soft, furry face against the boy's neck.

They all loved Misty. He made a little noise whenever he appeared, as if to introduce himself. Then he would either lie on the floor on his back and wait for his tummy to be tickled, or find a lap to curl up on and fall asleep.

Tonight, once they were inside the house, the cat sprang out of Robert's arms and headed for the kitchen to see if there was any food in his bowl.

He was in luck.

Mum had just taken the tin of cat food out of the fridge.

"Bet Misty will be allowed to watch 'Mr Finger's Downfall'," Robert said.

"That cat will be asleep," Dad laughed, "and no, Robert, you are not watching it. Neither is Jack."

"Why not?" Jack asked, coming down the stairs. He was two years older than Robert and was sometimes allowed to stay up and watch things on television after Robert had gone to bed. He had hoped he would be allowed to tonight.

"Because," Dad said, "it's been rated as a fifteen. That means there will be things in it that are not good for children your age to see."

"I'm nearly twelve," Jack said.

"But not yet," Dad said. "Sometimes there are things in a film that make the story more real. That is all right for adults to watch but at the moment, Mum and I think you're still too young to see them."

"Oh," Jack said. "All my friends watch them."

"And that's up to their parents to decide," Dad said. "You're going to have to trust Mum and me when we say you're too young."

Jack pulled a face but did not say anything else. They were disturbed, anyway, as the cat threw himself across the hall and into the front room. He had finished his food in one minute ten seconds, which was about normal, and was now making a dash for the comfy chair.

Mum followed him out of the kitchen.

"Hello, you two," she greeted them. "Which film did you choose?" she asked Robert.

Robert handed her the box with 'The Return of Dinky Robot' in it.

"Didn't we have a 'Dinky Robot' film out a while back?" she said. "It was quite good, I seem to remember. Tea's nearly ready."

She walked over to the video recorder and put the cassette in it.

"We'll eat in here. Jack, can you fetch the knives and forks from the kitchen for me? And Robert, can you bring in the drinks?"

"And try not to spill them," Dad said, remembering what had happened last time Robert had carried in a tray of drinks.

Chapter 2

The start of the play

Billy was clutching a brand new, bright blue pair of football boots when he came to school on Monday.

"My dad came yesterday," he grinned.

"Let's have a look then," Philip Hobson demanded. Charlie, Jack and Robert gathered round as well.

"Wish I had a pair like that," Charlie sighed.

"My dad says he'll get *me* a new pair if I score a goal in the match tonight," Philip said.

Why does Philip have to come to this school? Robert thought as Mr Bradbury

asked them all to sit down so that he could take the register.

Mr Bradbury was their teacher. He had taught them last year as well. He told terrible jokes, ran the school football team and sometimes gave them really hard work.

Like today.

"In our literacy work for the next couple of weeks," he began a few minutes later, "we're going to do something completely different."

Robert groaned. This sounded like bad news.

"Mrs Smith and I have decided that each of the Year Four classes are going to write a play," the teacher continued, "and if they're good enough, which they are going to be, we'll put them on for your parents. There'll be props to make, costumes to get ready, tickets to sell and loads of other things as well. You could even write a song if you wanted to."

"What are the plays going to be about?" Amy asked.

"That's for you to decide," Mr Bradbury answered. "Today you are going to write down your ideas."

A buzz of excitement ran round the class.

"You can work in groups or pairs or on your own," he carried on. "In your jotter books I want you to describe characters that could be in the play. Then you need to work out a story outline which will need a beginning, a middle and..."

"...an end," everyone joined in.

As usual, Billy and Robert worked together. They liked the thought of doing a play but had not got any ideas for what it should be about. So they started talking about tonight's football match instead.

"You two haven't written anything down yet," Mr Bradbury suddenly interrupted them. "Robert, what do you think the play should be about?"

Robert gulped.

He had not got a clue. He was not that bothered, either.

Suddenly he remembered 'The Return of Dinky Robot'.

"A robot that gets smashed up by these people and then mends itself and saves the world from some baddies," he said all in one breath.

Billy looked at his friend in amazement.

Mr Bradbury raised his eyebrows.

"Why haven't you written it all down then?" he asked.

"We were just about to," Billy chipped in, picking up his pencil.

"Okay then," Mr Bradbury said and moved on to the next table.

"Where did you get that from?" Billy whispered.

"Video we watched on Saturday night," Robert whispered back.

'Robot' Billy wrote at the top of his page and then paused. He hated writing almost as much as Robert did.

"Why don't we see if Charlie and Ashley will let us work with them?" he said, nodding his head towards the two boys working at the table behind them.

"What's their play about?" Robert said.

"There's one way to find out," Billy said.

Both boys leaned back on their chairs to listen.

"Flour," Charlie was saying, "what you make cakes with and flower like daffodils are."

"And blue like in the colour blue and blew if you blew up a balloon," Ashley added. "They're different words."

"Can we come and work with you?" Billy asked. "We've got an idea about a robot but don't know what to do with him."

Ashley and Charlie looked at each other.

"Mr Bradbury said we could work in groups if we wanted to," Billy added. "It'll be much better."

"All right, then," Ashley said.

Four brains were better than two, even if they did end up talking about football. But today, believe it or not, they got on with what they were supposed to be doing. Ashley could write really fast and before

long they had filled three whole pages with
their ideas.

"I'm looking forward to reading that,"
Mr Bradbury said at the end of the lesson
as he collected Ashley's jotter book in.
Then he spoke to the whole class.

"It's lunch time in a minute. Football
team, try not to injure yourselves, please."

Robert wished the butterfly in his tummy would go away. It had woken up again at the mention of tonight's football match.

Chapter 3

The first match

That afternoon they had science followed by quiet reading. The minute hand of the clock on the wall seemed to move more slowly than usual, but at last it read half past three and afternoon school was over. Six boys from the other Year Four class appeared clutching their football kit.

"Get changed quickly," Mr Bradbury said as he headed for the door. "I'm going to grab a cup of coffee from the staff-room. I'll be back in five minutes and I want you ready by then."

Lots of people, including some mums and dads, were gathering outside to watch the match and cheer for St George's School.

"Are your mum or dad coming?" Billy asked Robert.

Robert shook his head.

"No. Mum's got to work today until half past four and Dad said he was too busy."

He would have liked his mum and dad to have been there. They came sometimes, unlike Billy's mum who could never come to see him because she was always at work.

Robert got his boots out. They were still muddy from last time he had played. Mum had told him to clean them but he had not got round to it. They looked so tatty next to Billy's beautiful blue ones.

Philip Hobson scowled at Robert.

"Hope you're not going to miss the ball like you did last match," he said in a nasty voice. "I want to be captain of a team that wins, not loses. So you'd better make sure you play properly, or I'll get you afterwards."

Robert remembered missing the easy ball Charlie had kicked to him last time they

had played. Kingsmead School had picked it up and scored a goal from it. Trust Philip to remind him. Robert wanted to say something back but did not dare. Instead he looked down at his football boots and picked some dried mud off the studs.

"Who's the one with the lovely new boots then?" Mr Bradbury said to Billy as he came into the classroom a few minutes later.

"My dad bought them for me," Billy grinned.

"That's nice," the teacher said and gave Billy a special smile.

At that moment the team from Peterdown School arrived, dressed in their purple and white kit.

They were enormous!

One of the boys stared straight at Robert and pulled a nasty face. Robert looked at Billy to see if he had seen what the boy had done. Billy had not. He was too busy fiddling with the laces on his boots.

Mr Bradbury could not have seen it either. He was talking to Philip and the Peterdown captain. They were tossing the coin to decide which team would have first kick and which would choose ends.

I don't like this, Robert thought, as the boy pulled another face at him.

"Tails," Philip called out in a loud voice.

Mr Bradbury flipped a coin in the air. It landed on the floor.

"Heads," he announced.

Peterdown chose to kick off first.

Robert's heart was pounding as they

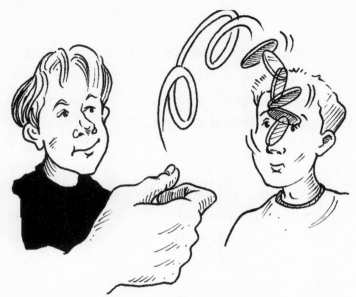

crossed the playground a few minutes later.

"My dad told me to choose tails," Philip said. "It's his fault we lost the toss, not mine. Anyway we were goi – "

He was cut off as four Peterdown boys ran alongside them.

"You wait," one of them sneered. "You'll all be crying your little eyes out by the time we've finished with you."

The boy spat on the ground and laughed.

Robert was actually glad Philip was with them. He waited for him to say something back.

But Philip said nothing and the four boys swaggered off, leaving Robert feeling even more scared than before. They reached the football pitch and kicked the ball around to warm themselves up until the Peterdown teacher called for them to get ready to start. Robert took up his position in mid-field.

"Come on!" shouted one of the mums from the side-line. "We want St George's to win!"

"Go for it, Peterdown!" another parent yelled back in reply. "Show 'em what you're made of."

"Hope I don't get too many bruises," Robert thought.

He wished *his* mum and dad were there. They would have asked God to look after him. Why couldn't he do the same?

"Dear God," he whispered, though not too loudly in case someone heard him, "help me play my best and not get hurt, especially if we win and they try to smash us up afterwards. Amen."

"And stop Philip being so nasty," he added.

Should he have said that last bit? Did God like that sort of thing?

Philip *was* nasty. God must know that already, so he wasn't telling him anything new and he must concentrate on his football now.

The ball seemed to go from one end of the pitch to the other with neither side being able to score. Even Philip could not get the ball round the boy who was marking him.

"You've got to ignore how tall they are," Mr Bradbury told them at half-time. "Just go for the ball."

Five minutes later, Philip did just that. He suddenly dribbled the ball round several players and booted it straight at the Peterdown keeper. The keeper nearly managed to hold on to it but as the ball rolled out of his arms Philip chipped it in to the back of the net.

"Yes!" he shouted as the supporters on the touch-line cheered.

"Well done, Philip!" Mr Bradbury called out. "You deserved that one."

He's got his new football boots as well, Robert thought as they ran back to their starting positions.

Boring!

But it *was* nice to be on the winning side, so maybe having Philip on your team was not all bad!

Then Peterdown equalised.

Robert was thankful they had not scored from a mistake he had made, but every ball mattered now and time was ticking away.

With eight minutes to go Philip fell over and made a real fuss about it.

Get up! Robert thought, as Philip lay on the ground and Mr Bradbury rubbed his leg and gave him a drink.

Eventually Philip staggered to his feet and St George's was given a free kick which Billy took. The ball went straight to Philip who did another amazing dribble followed by a shot at goal which nearly went in.

So much for being hurt, Robert thought.

There were only five minutes to go.

"Come on, someone," Robert sighed. "Get a goal."

As if hearing him, Simon Jennings from Mrs Smith's class suddenly sent the ball floating across the pitch to where Billy was and the next thing Robert knew, the whistle had gone because the ball was in the back of the Peterdown net.

"Must be Billy's new boots," Charlie laughed.

Robert smiled. He wanted the game to end now, especially as the Peterdown team seemed to be getting rougher and tougher with every passing second. His elbow was throbbing where he'd been at the wrong end of a tackle earlier on. He had a quick look at it to see if it was bleeding.

"Wake up, Robert!" Charlie yelled.

A purple and white body dribbling a football was pounding down the pitch towards him. It had already got past John and left him lying on the ground.

Robert held his breath.

He knew he had to get this right. If they scored because he made a mistake, he might have Philip as well as the Peterdown team wanting to smash him up afterwards. He concentrated on the ball and tried to ignore the enormous boy behind it.

Now! he thought and slammed his boot as hard as he could against the leather ball. A body swung hard into his chest and left him gasping for breath.

"Good tackle!" he heard someone shout as the ball spun away towards Charlie. Robert thought he recognised the voice and looked up to see... his dad!

Robert waved to him.

Dad had said he had too much on to come and watch. But he had come after all. At least if Peterdown caused any trouble, his Dad would make sure nothing happened to him.

Robert breathed a sigh of relief.

He breathed another one two minutes later when the final whistle blew and Philip called out, "Three cheers for Peterdown."

"Hooray," Robert whispered, more because the game was over than for the other team. Apart from his elbow, he was not injured, either.

"Well played," Mr Bradbury said as the group of muddy, breathless boys gathered round him. "And well done for not getting too rough."

Robert looked at the Peterdown boys. They were heading for the table where drinks and biscuits had been put out.

"Bet there won't be any biscuits or drink left for us," someone said.

Robert did not mind if there wasn't.

"You played well in the few minutes I was watching," Dad said as they walked across the field back to the classroom.

Then he leaned over and whispered something.

"Brill!" Robert grinned. "I'll just get my bags from the classroom. Be back in a minute."

Chapter 4

Misty

Dad had told Robert that Uncle Jim was staying for tea.

Uncle Jim was Robert's favourite uncle. He ran the 'Cover Your Floor Store' in town and often dropped in to see them when he was delivering carpets to houses nearby.

"Did you win?" Uncle Jim greeted them.

"Yup. 2-1," Robert answered.

"Did you score any of the goals?"

"He plays in defence," Mum said, "so I hope he didn't. He did last match and wasn't very popular."

"Philip scored one and Billy scored the

other," Robert said, dropping his coat on the floor and heading for the fridge.

"Excuse me," Mum said. "Does your coat like pretending to be a carpet?"

"I could lay it in a tiny room I've got to fit tomorrow," Uncle Jim laughed. "Might need stretching a bit though."

He looked at his nephew and winked.

"Jim," Mum said, "don't encourage him. I've just got in from work and I'm tired. I don't want him, or you, making a mess on the floor which *I* might have to tidy up."

"I'll hang it up in a minute, after I've had a drink of milk," Robert said, then looked up as someone knocked on the back door. It was Mrs Wills from next door.

"Can you come?" she whispered urgently to Mum.

"Okay," Mum said with a frown, "and when I get back," she added over her shoulder, "that coat will be hung up in its proper place, won't it Robert?"

"Now you've been told," Uncle Jim laughed.

Robert finished his drink and was about to raid the cake tin when Mum came back in. She had blood on the back of her hands.

She took a deep breath.

"Misty's been hit by a car," she said, fighting back the tears.

"Where?" Dad asked.

"Outside," she whispered. Her lips moved but little sound came out.

"He's dead."

"He can't be!" Robert said. "I saw him at breakfast time this morning."

All the excitement of the day disappeared. Misty was part of home, part of the family.

He couldn't be dead.

Not Misty.

Not the cat.

A sharp pain twisted inside his stomach and he felt tears welling up in his eyes.

"I'll go and tell Jack," Dad said and left the room.

"Come here, love," Mum said and held her arms out. Robert crossed the room and sank his face into her warm shoulder and began sobbing.

"He's at the side of the road," Mum whispered to Dad when he came back in the kitchen. Jack was with him, tears streaming down his face.

"Right," Dad said to Uncle Jim. "Can you come and help me? We've got a horrible job to do." Dad was having difficulty speaking because he was crying too. He bent over and picked up Misty's blanket from the basket by the sink.

"Can I come too?" Jack sniffed.

Dad looked at Mum.

"It's not very nice," she said quietly, "but if you really want to, then you can."

Jack moved across and took Dad's hand.

"I'm not going," Robert said. "I don't want to see it."

"That's sensible," Mum whispered.

Robert heard the cat flap rattle as the back door shut behind them. Misty would never come through it again.

"I'm going to miss him," Robert whispered.

"We all will," Mum said, wiping her eyes with the back of her sleeve.

Before long they heard footsteps trudging past the back door. They were carrying a little bundle wrapped in a blanket.

"Shall we go and see?" Mum whispered. "We need to say 'goodbye' to Misty. I'll get my coat. It's cold out there."

Robert picked *his* coat up off the floor and together they went outside to where the others were and stared at the mound inside the blanket lying on the patio. Mum bent down and carefully pulled back one corner. The half-light from the kitchen window shone across the cat's face.

"Do you want to give him one last stroke?" she asked.

Robert crouched down.

So did Jack.

They gently stroked Misty's forehead and tickled his chin but there was no purring or nuzzling into their hands like there would have been a few hours before.

"Goodbye Misty," Jack whispered.

Robert wanted to say the same thing but couldn't get the words out.

"We'll dig a hole near his favourite bush and bury him there," Dad said, opening the shed door to get the spades out.

Jack, Robert and Mum stood still, listening to the harsh sound of metal hitting soil.

"I'm hurting," Mum said in an empty sort of voice. "Sometimes you don't realise how much you love something or someone until they've gone."

Robert sniffed.

"I wish today had never happened," he said as Misty's body was carefully lowered in to the hole.

Mum put her hand on his shoulder.

"Thank you, God, for Misty," she whispered.

"Will Misty be in heaven?" Jack asked.

"*People* go to heaven," Mum said, "but no one knows for certain whether or not animals go there as well."

They stood in silence for a few minutes.

"Why did Misty have to get run over?" Robert asked as another wave of sadness exploded inside him.

"I don't know," Mum sighed. "Things happen and we don't know why. We have to trust God that he knows what he's doing and ask him to help us get through sad times. He knows how you're feeling at the moment..."

"I just feel..." Robert started to say. Only he did not finish the sentence. Instead he buried his head in Mum's coat and cried and cried.

Five minutes later Uncle Jim and Dad finished filling in the hole they had just dug.

Chapter 5

The play takes shape

A sad feeling settled on the whole family for the next few days. Dad sealed up the cat flap and put Misty's basket in the loft. Mrs Wills from next door baked them a chocolate cake to try and cheer them up.

"Are you going to get another cat?" she asked as she dropped the cake off.

"Maybe one day, but not at the moment," Mum replied.

She and Dad were missing Misty as much as Robert and Jack were.

"Forward," she said on Monday morning at breakfast time. "A new week is ahead of us."

Robert let out a long sigh. At least he was not hurting quite as much as he had done last week.

"Wonder whose ideas Mr Bradbury has decided to use for the play," Billy said as he and Robert walked to school in drizzling rain.

With everything else, Robert had completely forgotten about the play.

"It's been very difficult choosing," Mr Bradbury announced half an hour later. "You came up with such wonderful ideas. Eventually I decided that Ashley, Charlie, Robert and Billy's was the best. Theirs had lots of action, and a good beginning, middle..."

"...and end," everyone joined in.

Robert felt a grin spread right across his face as Mr Bradbury picked up a pile of photocopied sheets and asked Amy to give them out.

"Here are some ideas for the first scene which we're going to have a go at writing today," he said. "I'll go through the sheet with you first, then you can work in your groups."

INTRODUCTION

SCENE ONE BREAKFAST TIME IN THE KITCHEN

THINK ABOUT
Which other characters are in the play?

Who are they? Give them names.

Introduce them.

Introduce the robot.

Where has he come from?

Why is he there?

How does he speak?

What does he do?

ACTION
It is breakfast time and the robot appears.

What does everybody think of him?

The children start trying to make him talk.

How?

By the end of the session they had a long list of words with double meanings for the robot to muddle up. Amy had been chosen to be the robot and Hannah and Philip – being the tallest in the class – were going to play Mum and Dad. Billy and Becky were to be the two children and Charlie was to be the narrator. No one could think of a really good name for the robot so Mr Bradbury said they would leave it for the time being. Maybe they would have a competition to decide later on.

Trust Philip to get one of the main parts, Robert thought. He gets everything. Captain of the football team, new pair of boots and now a big part in the play.

But no one really likes him, Robert thought later as Philip was sent to the back of the line – yet again – by the dinner lady. He had not been able to find a partner as the class lined up to go across to the dining hall for lunch.

He very rarely did.

Chapter 6

Cucumber arrives

Mr Bradbury paused and looked round. Everyone had just voted to decide what to call the robot. There had been three favourites, so they had all had a piece of paper and written down their choice.

"In third place was 'Robo' with five votes," Mr Bradbury said.

Colin pulled a face. That had been his name.

"In second place with nine votes was the name 'Ticker'... but the winner was... 'Meep'."

Charlie grinned. That had been his idea.

So the play was to be called 'Meep Comes to Earth' and over the next few weeks it was sometimes talked about even more than football. Unless, of course, there was an important match coming up. Then they talked about that instead.

Mr Bradbury bought a new match football for them to play with *and* a new kit for them to wear. It had its first outing for the match against Hillford Primary School which they won 3-4.

St George's really were playing well as a team and Mr Bradbury's grin got bigger with every match they played.

"Well done!" he always said. "I've never had a team like you lot! You just keep on winning!"

Robert was made man of the match after the cup game against Glenfield Primary. Being man of the match meant he kept a little trophy for the following week. It sat on the kitchen window sill and Mum took a photograph of him holding it to send to Gran.

And in between all this, the play continued to take shape.

Once the script was finished, everyone had a go at typing a little bit out on one of the school computers. Each character was given a different font. Robert kept forgetting to change fonts and had to type most of his bit twice.

Then there was scenery, lighting, costumes, props, advertising, sound effects and loads of other things to think about as well. Robert had not realised so much had to be done to put on a play. He and Hasan were in charge of the props so had to find things that the actors needed when they were on stage.

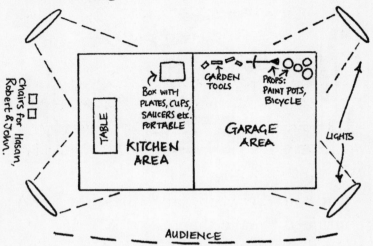

The stage was divided into two main areas, the kitchen and the garage. Dad helped Robert sort out things like paint pots and gardening tools for the garage part. He brought them to school one afternoon after he had finished his milk round.

Mr Bradbury had a word with the reception class teacher who said they could borrow anything they liked from her classroom. Hasan and Robert collected the toy sink first. Then they fetched saucepans and knives and forks and spoons and jugs and bowls and loads of other things. They put them in a large plastic box at the back of the hall.

There were to be two performances of the play: one on Wednesday afternoon for the rest of the school to watch – that was like a dress rehearsal – and one on Thursday evening for parents.

The tickets for the evening performance were printed off on the computer. They were going to charge for that performance and raise some money for charity. Mr Bradbury suggested 86p for each ticket. That was to make them do difficult sums. Nobody, apart from Nicola and Tom, who were both brilliant at maths, agreed with him.

So after a class vote the tickets were priced at £1. That was much more sensible!

Robert bought three.

One for Mum, one for Dad and one for Jack.

You are invited to watch

'Meep Comes to Earth' by 4B

and

'Eskimo Ice' by 4S

☆ ☆ ☆ ☆

Time   6.15
Date   Thursday 10th April
Place   St George's School hall
Price   £1.00

The day Robert came out of school clutching his tickets, Mum was waiting for him. That was unusual. It *was* a Thursday and she did not work on a Thursday, but since he had been at junior school Robert had always walked home on his own.

"Dad's in the car," she said in a mysterious voice when he reached her, but she would not tell him where they were going.

54

They drove to Jack's school first and picked him up.

"What's going on?" Jack kept on asking. "Where are you taking us?"

"Just wait," Mum kept saying.

The car drew up outside an old house about two miles away and Dad switched off the engine.

"Here we are," he said.

"'Cat Rescue Centre'," Jack read from a board on the side of the house.

"I called in here on Tuesday," Mum said, "and saw a beautiful ginger cat. He's called 'Cucumber'. What about that for a name? Poor thing's been ill-treated. Dad saw him yesterday and, like me, thinks he's gorgeous. We've brought you to have a look at him today to see what you think."

"Is that him?" Robert asked a few minutes later, pointing to a large ball of ginger fur curled up in the corner of a large cardboard box.

The man from the Rescue Centre nodded.

Mum squatted down next to the box.

"Hello Cucumber," she whispered gently, and began picking him up. He spat at her and dug his claws into her shoulder. Mum kept hold of him.

"It's all right," she whispered gently. "I won't let you fall."

There was definitely something special about him, apart from his name. His fur was such a fantastic colour and his tail was ever so long.

Robert put his hand out to stroke him.

Cucumber hissed and dug his front paws harder into Mum's shoulder. There was a wild expression in his eyes.

"Ow!" Mum mouthed, but she did not let go even though the cat was hurting her.

"You just need someone to love you, don't you?" she whispered. "Then you'll calm down."

They stood watching as Mum soothed the cat.

"What do you think?" Dad said.

"Will he sit on my lap like Misty used to?" Robert asked.

"In time," Mum said, "but not to start with."

Cucumber had given up struggling with Mum and just looked sadly at them.

"Let's have him," Jack said.

Robert felt his head nodding in agreement.

"Good," Mum said. "Dad and I hoped you'd say that. We could change his name if you wanted to."

"No, I like the name 'Cucumber'," Jack said.

"So do I," Robert agreed.

Dad went to get Misty's old carrier cage

from the boot of their car. Mum got out her cheque book to give a donation to the Rescue Centre. Then they set off home.

Cucumber was not a happy cat. He spat and hissed and tried to scratch the sides of the carrier cage. Then he just gave up and cowered at the back, staring out at them.

"He needs time and lots of love," Mum said later as she put a plaster over a deep scratch on Jack's hand.

"I only wanted to stroke him," Jack said.

"He's still scared of you," Mum said. "He *will* come round but he's got to learn to trust you first."

"God," Robert prayed that night as he lay in bed, "help us do the right things to help Cucumber. Amen."

"And help Philip become nicer as well," he added. He always put that bit in when he or anyone else prayed.

He thought about when the Peterdown football team were being nasty to them and he had prayed and Dad had turned up to watch the match.

Was that God answering his prayer?

Would God answer his prayers about the cat and about Philip as well?

He would have to wait and see.

Chapter 7

The day of the play

At last it was Wednesday, the day of the play.

Robert woke up feeling excited and nervous all at the same time, and he was not even one of the actors. What must they be feeling like?

This week was turning into one of the most exciting weeks in the whole of his life. Yesterday they had played Wellington Junior School in the semi-finals of the football cup.

And won.

Robert had nearly scored a goal – for his own team, not the opposition. Only his shot had missed. He should not really have been so far forward, but no one seemed to mind.

The end score was an amazing five-one. That meant they were through to the final. The other semi-final, between Farringdon and Manor Court Primary, was being played tonight.

Robert got out of bed and went downstairs. Cucumber ignored him. He lay in his basket and watched what was going on. At least he did not spit and hiss at him any more which was something.

On his way to school, Robert called for Billy as usual.

"Guess what," Billy greeted him, his eyes shining with excitement. "My dad phoned last night and he's promised to come and see me in the play. Mum's got to work late so couldn't come. Dad says we'll go out for a burger afterwards as well."

Robert smiled.

He was really pleased for his friend.

That morning, Mr Bradbury gave up trying to get them to be quiet and do any work. He gave them a sheet of puzzles to do instead.

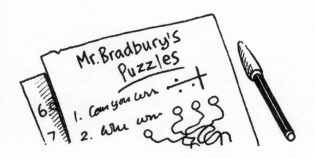

Eventually afternoon school began and it was time to get ready. Amy's costume was a large box covered in two layers of paper which had been sprayed with silver paint. She had just put it on when Robert and Hasan left the classroom to take up their positions next to John at the right of the stage.

John was the prompter. His job was to follow the script in case one of the actors forgot their words. He was flicking through the sheets on his clipboard and had just reached the kitchen scene with the eggs and flour in it. They'd always practised this part by pretending, but today Mr Bradbury had brought in *real* eggs and *real* flour for them to use. Robert looked over John's shoulder.

(*All move to the kitchen table where flour, sugar, eggs and margarine are laid out.*)
BILLY   Meep, this is a spoon. Say spoon.
MEEP   Spoon.
BECKY   And this is a table. Say table.
MEEP   Table.

MUM   Are you lot going to help me make this cake or not?

BILLY   Eggs, flour, margarine, sugar. *(points to each of them)* Can you say that, Meep?

MEEP   Eggs, flour, margarine, sugar.

BECKY   Mum, did you hear her? Isn't she getting good at talking? Say them again, Meep.

MEEP   Eggs, flour, margarine, sugar.

MUM   What a clever little robot you are.

(Mum puts sugar and margarine in mixing bowl)

MUM   Can she say all the letters of the alphabet yet?

BECKY   Listen to this, Mum. We'll start at the end instead of the beginning. Z.

MEEP   Z

BECKY   Y

MEEP   Y

BECKY   What's next, Meep?

(Meep picks up two eggs)

MEEP   X... X

(Meep throws an egg each at Becky and Billy)

MUM   Meep, stop it! Why are you throwing eggs round the kitchen?

BILLY   She thinks eggs are X.

MUM   Oh Meep, you silly thing. Look at the mess you've made. You two go and get your clothes changed while I tidy up. Now sit there Meep and don't move.

(Billy and Becky exit. Mum puts the cake in the oven and the bowl in the sink.)

MUM   Right Meep. You can come with me. In a minute I'm going in to the garden to pick some flowers to put in the jug.

(Mum puts the jug on the table. Meep picks up the flour and empties it all over

the jug and table.)
MUM   Oy! What are you doing now?
MEEP   Flour in jug on table.

"I love that bit," John whispered.

"Best bit. It'll make a right mess if Amy does it right," Hasan giggled.

When she actually did do it, the audience loved it too. They were laughing so much that they nearly missed the next bit. Meep discovered a cartoon character on the television who lived in a garden and was called 'Green Fingers'. Of course, Meep wanted to have *her* fingers painted green as well.

So Becky and Billy took her to the garage. Julie got the lighting just right. The 'kitchen' was plunged into darkness as the 'garage' part of the stage became floodlit.

Then everyone started laughing again as Billy and Becky painted Meep's top silver layer of paper green! They did not just do her fingers either.

Robert looked at the large sheet of plastic that had been laid on the stage blocks to protect them from the eggs and the flour and now the paint. Mr Bradbury had been a bit worried it would slip when people started walking on it, but it seemed to be holding all right.

John quietly turned a page of the script over. He was following it very closely, just in case someone forgot their lines.

BECKY   But she only wanted her fingers green.
BILLY   But you like being painted, don't you, Meep?
MEEP   Green fingers! Green feet! Me like green!

Robert kept reading as John moved his fingers down the script.

NARRATOR   The children did not know that there were chemicals in the paint. These made Meep become very ill and it wasn't long before their little friend lay still on the ground.

BILLY   Speak to me Meep. Say something.

MEEP   Meep not feel good.

BECKY   What shall we do?

BILLY   Better get Mum and Dad.

So Hannah and Philip came on the stage to see what was going on. They decided the only way to save Meep was to rip the layer of green paint off.

Robert looked at the audience. The reception class, sitting on the front row, hardly moved. Most of them had their mouths open, waiting to see what would happen next.

The wet layer of green paper was peeled off and put in a bin bag. But Meep still lay on the floor.

BECKY I think we've killed her.
MEEP No you haven't! Me okay now! Meep not dead anymore! But don't paint me again.

At this point, Mrs Horner began playing the piano and everyone in the class stood up to sing the song they had written. It was about looking after each other and the world they lived in. Then Meep did a little dance before getting in to a huge cardboard box which was made to look like a space ship.

And that was it. They had done their play and everyone was clapping. Mr Bradbury thanked them for being such a wonderful audience. Then he thanked the class for working so hard to put the play on and everyone clapped again.

A short interval followed while the stage blocks were cleared and the plastic sheeting was cleaned up and put away for tomorrow's performance. Mrs Smith's class got ready to put on their play. It was about a family of Eskimos whose igloo kept on melting.

Billy, Robert and the rest of class 4B (including Mr Bradbury, only he was not allowed to say so because he was a teacher) all thought it was a very boring play compared to theirs.

Robert couldn't wait to get home so he could tell Dad all about it.

"It was fantastic," he finished, "especially the bit where Amy threw the eggs and tipped flour all over the place. We didn't think Mr Bradbury would let her do it with the real things, but he did."

Then he suddenly added, "Where's the cat?"

"In the lounge, I think," Dad said. "But don't disturb him."

"I won't," Robert sighed, but he wanted to see Cucumber anyway, just to make sure he was all right.

The cat was stretched out on the settee. He stared at Robert but did not jump up and run away like he used to. Neither did that wild look come in his eyes.

"Hello!" Robert whispered. "Is today going to be the day you let me stroke you without getting scratched?"

Cucumber watched as the boy slowly moved towards him.

Robert waited for a front paw to lash out at him.

Only it did not.

Very carefully, he let his fingers rest on the warm fur. The cat's body stiffened for a few seconds, then relaxed.

Ever so slowly, ever so gently, Robert moved his hand down the animal's back.

"Aren't you soft?" he murmured. "Are you going to let me pick you up as well?"

"No, Robert," Dad said from behind him. "Let the cat be. He's let you stroke him today. That's enough. Don't overdo it."

"Okay," Robert whispered. "I'm glad Cucumber came to live with us."

Dad just smiled.

"So am I," he said.

Chapter 8

The second performance

The first thing Mr Bradbury told them the following morning was that the football team would be playing Farringdon Junior School in the cup final. He also told them that Farringdon had won every single match they had played so far that season.

"But you're all playing really well at the moment," he said, "and I think you can win. But we have other things to do before the match. Like putting on a play!"

No one ever quite knew how it happened. Maybe it was a bit of egg from the cake-making scene that dripped off Billy's jumper. Maybe Philip did not watch where he was putting his foot.

They had reached the final scene and Robert remembered hearing Amy cry out "me okay now!"

But the next thing he knew, Philip had slipped off the staging blocks and was sprawled across the floor, holding his ankle.

The audience leaned forward to see what had happened and Mr Bradbury hurried to the front. Philip looked as though he was in real pain, not like when he was on the football pitch and put it on. He was carried off to the secretary's office and they had to finish the play without him.

It rather spoiled it. As they sang their song and watched Meep get in the cardboard spaceship, there was not the excitement there had been the previous day.

Especially amongst the football team.

Philip was one of their best players and even though they did not always like him, they had a cup final game on Saturday week to think about.

Robert, who was standing next to Billy, was suddenly aware his friend was crying.

What's up with him? Robert thought. He's not *that* friendly with Philip.

Then he thought of something else and as Mr Bradbury made his little speech about how wonderful they all were, his eyes scanned the audience.

Billy's dad was not there.

Robert did not know what to say to Billy.

So he said nothing.

What he did do though was stay by his friend as lots of mums and dads came to say "well done" and stretch their legs before 'Eskimo Ice' began.

"What's up?" Mum asked Billy when she and Dad came to see Robert.

"My dad didn't come," Billy said, wiping his face with the back of his hand. It was still green from when they had painted Meep. "He promised he would. We were going out afterwards as well."

"Oh Billy," Mum said and put her arm round his shoulders. "I know we're not the same as your own mum or dad, but we thought you were brilliant."

Billy sniffed.

"Do you want to come with *us* afterwards?" Dad said. "We've promised Jack we'll go to the fish and chip shop on the way home."

Billy nodded and wiped his face with the back of his other hand. That, too, had green paint on it.

"Shall Robert go with you to wash your hands?" Mum said.

Billy nodded.

By the time they came back from the toilets everyone was starting to settle down to watch 'Eskimo Ice'. An announcement was made to say that Philip had been taken to hospital.

"If he's off school tomorrow, are you going to send him a card to say you hope he gets better quickly?" Mum asked as they walked across to the car later on.

"No way!" Robert replied.

Mum raised her eyebrows.

"I think you should," she said. "I know you don't like him very much, but how would you like it if it happened to you?"

"He won't be able to play football if he's broken his leg," Billy said. "We'd miss him then."

"Maybe he hasn't broken it," Jack said in a big brother sort of voice, "and he might be back tomorrow."

"Let's hope so," Mum said.

They did not mention Philip again. After their fish and chips they took Billy round to his house. His mum had just got in. Dad explained what had happened. Billy's mum said something very rude.

"I wish I could do something to help Billy," Robert said later on as he got ready for bed.

"He was hurting inside, wasn't he?" Dad said. "He'll still be hurting tomorrow as well. Shall we ask God to let you know how to help him?"

Robert nodded.

And stop Philip being so nasty, Robert added to himself as Dad finished.

The next morning Mr Bradbury looked very fed up. Philip's leg was broken and he would be off school for at least a fortnight. When he *did* come back his leg would be in plaster. There was no way he would be playing football on Saturday week. Not only had Mr Bradbury lost one of his best football players, but Philip's dad had been up to school and had a go at him for letting children use real eggs and flour that had made the floor slippery.

Philip's dad was not very pleasant at the best of times. He was even worse when he was angry.

"Robert, I'm thinking of making you captain of the football team," Mr Bradbury said. "If you move up to play where Philip usually plays, Amar from Mrs Smith's class can play in your place. Is that all right?"

Of course it was!

Robert went bright red with pleasure. Everyone seemed to be smiling at him.

That day, instead of talking about the play, they talked about the match and how they were going to manage without Philip.

But could they win without him?

Robert did not think so.

Neither did the others, if they were honest.

Chapter 9

At the end

On the day of the under-ten football cup final Dad got up at four o'clock instead of half past four. He reckoned if he started his milk round early, he could probably catch the last twenty minutes of the game.

Robert got up early too, though not as early as Dad, because he could not sleep. At five minutes to eleven, the players from St George's and Farringdon were on the pitch ready to start.

But Robert was worried.

Mr Bradbury was worried.

In fact, the whole of the St George's team was worried.

Because Billy had not arrived.

Robert had called for him earlier and his Mum had said he was not quite ready and if Robert went on Billy would come as soon as possible. She had looked really stressed.

At two minutes to eleven a figure appeared running towards the pitch.

"Here he is," someone shouted.

Everyone cheered and Billy gave a little wave.

"Captains," Farringdon's teacher called out.

Robert ran across and shook hands with the other captain who was going to call the toss. Mr Bradbury flicked the coin high in the air.

"Tails."

Robert watched the coin cartwheel through the air.

"Heads," Mr Bradbury announced. "Robert, you win. Which do you want, choice of ends or first kick off?"

"First kick-off please," Robert said. He was enjoying being captain.

"Right you are then," Farringdon's teacher said. "And may the best team win."

Hope that's us, Robert thought.

Farringdon played well. They had good control of the ball and passed accurately to each other. But they lacked speed up front and St George's managed to keep up a steady pressure on the Farringdon defence and deserved the goal Pete scored just before half-time.

"Fantastic," Robert thought. "That cup will be ours and I'll have been the captain of the team that won." A thrill of excitement ran down his spine and he looked over to where his mum was standing to make sure she was still there.

She was, and someone was standing next to her, resting on a pair of crutches.

"Seen Philip?" Robert called to Billy as they ran back to their starting positions.

"No, where is he?" Billy asked.

"By my mum," Robert replied, and pointed across to where she was standing.

Just then the whistle blew and they had to concentrate on the game again. They needed to as well for Farringdon had made a substitution. The boy who had come on was better than the rest of the team put together. He dribbled and passed and chipped and very nearly managed to score just as the whistle went for half time.

"You're playing really well," Mr Bradbury said. "But you'll have to watch that boy who's just come on. Stick with him especially when he's near the goal mouth. And have you seen who's over there?" he added.

Mr Bradbury nodded towards where Philip was standing. "Do some of you want to run across and say 'hello' to him? You've got a few minutes before we start playing again."

"Bet he'll find something wrong with what we're doing," Robert said as he, Billy, Charlie and Simon jogged across to where Philip was standing.

"He'll probably say that if he'd been

87

playing the score would be three nil instead of one nil," Amar groaned.

"Five nil, don't you mean?" Charlie sighed.

But they were in for a shock.

Philip grinned at them.

Yes, he grinned.

"Thanks for the cards," he said to Billy and Robert and smiled at them again.

"That's all right," Billy said.

"Is your leg hurting a lot?" Simon asked.

"Not as much as it did at first," he said. "Wish I was playing today. But come on. Let's have another goal. You've got to win."

Was this really Philip? Robert thought.

Mum leaned over and straightened Robert's shirt collar. He pulled a face and ruffled it up again.

"You'd better go back and see if Mr Bradbury has got anything else to say to you," she said to them.

"See you later, Philip," Charlie called out as they turned and began walking back to where the rest of the team were squatting down. Simon and Charlie ran on ahead, leaving Robert and Billy behind.

Robert looked at his friend.

"You all right?" he asked.

"Yup!" Billy snapped.

No you're not, Robert thought.

Something was up, of that Robert was certain. Should he say something else?

He decided not to.

It was Farringdon who scored next. The boy who had been brought on just before half time dribbled the ball from the half way line, and then booted it so hard no one saw it until it was in the back of the net.

One all.

"Come on, St George's, we can still do it," Robert shouted as they prepared to kick off again.

But from then on everything fell apart. Try as they might, St George's could not even get the ball into Farringdon's half, let alone have a shot at goal.

That boy seemed to be everywhere and

five minutes later Farringdon scored again.
Same boy.
Same speed.
Two one.

Robert kept looking at Billy. He was not playing very well. Robert had to cover for him several times after he fumbled the ball. Something was up.

And then Farringdon scored again.

Same boy.

Same speed.

They could not touch him!

Three one.

"Come on St George's, let's get one back!" Robert panted as they jogged back to their starting positions, yet again.

"Why are we bothering?" Billy said. He stubbed the toe of his blue football boot hard into the turf and looked down.

"At least he didn't take my football boots," he muttered.

"What?" Robert said, catching the last few words.

"That's all he's left me," Billy spat at him. "He's gone to live a long way away. Went last week instead of coming to see me in the play. He phoned this morning and told Mum. She says he's never coming back and doesn't ever want to see her, or me, again."

Robert stared at Billy.

"Your dad's gone for ever?" he said.

He could not believe it.

Billy nodded.

"For ever," he whispered again.

Robert heard his own dad's voice.

"Come on, Robert!" he yelled. "You've got five minutes left. Stop talking and get a goal will you?"

But it was no use.

The final score was three one.

Mr Bradbury had bought some crisps, chocolate biscuits and lemonade for after the match, but what Mr Bradbury had hoped would be a happy party turned into a group of tired, muddy boys who wanted to get home as soon as possible.

Especially Billy.

He sat on the ground and stared at the grass as the tears rolled down his cheeks and onto his knees. Only Robert knew why *he* cried more than the others. And Robert just sat by him and said nothing.

That evening, Robert felt really fed up. There was not even much that was good on the television tonight. He was still going to watch it though. He was too tired to do anything else. The only good thing about today was that Philip had been nice.

Everything else had been bad.

Really bad.

Robert stretched out his tired legs and wished the day was over as a ginger ball of fur appeared by his side.

"Hello," he said gently, as Cucumber placed his front paws on his legs and then climbed on to his lap.

"Hello, Cucumber," Robert whispered again, tickling him behind the ears. The cat looked up at him, and, for the first time

Robert heard a little purring noise.

"What are you saying to me, little cat?" he whispered.

Ever so carefully, ever so slowly, he hugged the ball of fur. Cucumber did not strain to get away, but closed his eyes and pretended to be asleep. He was still there half an hour later when the phone rang. Mum answered it. Then she appeared at the lounge door.

"Look where the little cat is," Robert whispered, pointing at his lap.

"At last!" Mum said. "Something else has happened as well." She had an enormous grin on her face.

"Now," she whispered. "Keep calm and don't disturb the cat when I tell you what the phone call was about."

Robert looked at her.

"That was Mr Bradbury on the phone," she said. "You know that boy who scored all the goals this morning?"

Robert nodded.

How could he forget him?

"Well, Mr Bradbury overheard one of the Farringdon parents say that that boy is in Year Five at school."

"But we're all in Year Four," Robert interrupted.

"So, Mr Bradbury checked and what he overheard was right. So he's phoned up the people who organised the cup competition and told them. And they've decided that all the goals the boy scored are to be disallowed and that Farringdon can't enter the cup competition next year."

"But that boy scored *all* the goals," Robert gasped.

"Which means," Mum finished, "that St George's have won the cup!"

Robert did not know what to do first. He wanted to scream and jump up and down and shout and make a lot of noise. But he could not because Cucumber was pretending to be asleep on his lap.

"And on Monday," Mum finished, "you, as captain of the under-ten football team, will be presented with the cup in assembly."

Life was getting better by the minute!

What a day!

"Thank you for Cucumber," Robert whispered later that evening as he lay in bed. "Thank you that we won the cup. And be with Billy tonight."

Then he added, "and be with Philip as well."